THE PIGMENT THIEF

Myka Silber

Library and Archives Canada Cataloguing in Publication is available upon request.

ISBN: 978-1-7390571-3-8 (paperback)
ISBN: 978-1-7390571-4-5 (e-book)

Cover design and illustrations by Michelle Schumacher

Trash Panda Publications

OTHER TITLES
BY MYKA SILBER

INDIVIDUAL PUBLICATIONS

Soft & Rage: A Short Story Collection
Rider's Blood, Moonlit Black

ANTHOLOGIES

Unleash the Cosmos
(Nathaniel Luscombe & Jenni Sauer)

For anyone who's ever wanted to
throw a shoe at their ex.

PART
ONE

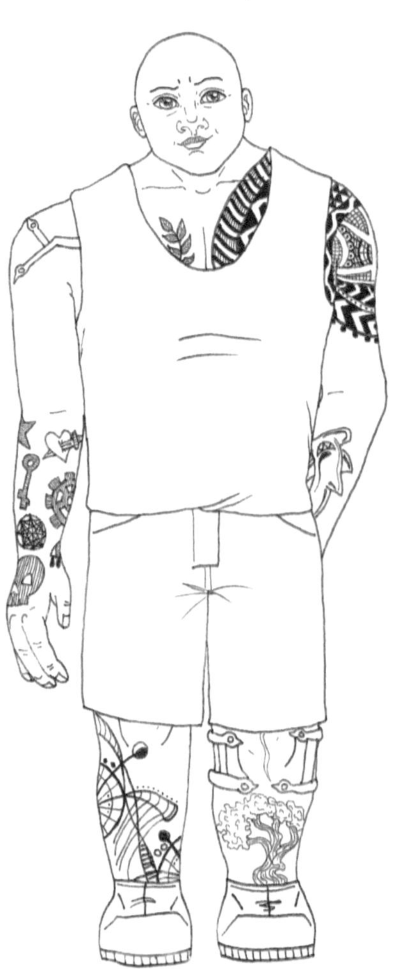

The fixer's hologram is not my favourite. It's a neon yellow cartoon rabbit bobblehead with an expression that cycles every few seconds. Too on the nose for someone called Rabbit. I only take it seriously because it's also expensive anti-AI obfuscation tech. The rest of their outfit could belong to anybody; just a black baggy jumpsuit that masks any details about them. No matter how secure a comms channel is, there's always a way in. Better safe than sorry.

I can't be bothered with anything that fancy — a standard black balaclava, mirrored sunglasses, an oversized parka, and a voice modulator that makes me sound like a middle-aged chain-smoking man over a normal hologram upload link is good enough for me. AI can't defeat the physical yet.

"C'mon Rabbit, no one's paying to get into the Scitek HQ building. It's a fortress. They've got their own private security and everything."

Rabbit's expression is now two x's for eyes. "You're the best art thief in North City. If anyone can do it, it's you."

True, but not convincing — maybe because most underworld operatives don't work art jobs. "I don't do corporate espionage."

Especially not when experimental tech might be involved. I'm the best because I don't take stupid risks.

"It's not corporate espionage, AgentLOL. Like I said, it's an art heist. Your specialty."

"How does the client even know the piece is in the building?"

Rabbit glitches for a moment, tipping me off that they're on two calls at once. When the hologram has stabilized, Rabbit says, "They've seen it themselves. It's on the 112th floor."

I whistle in admiration. "You've got expensive clients, Rabbit. No one gets that high in the HQ without being a gold-blood."

"Business is good," says Rabbit, their expression cycling from a laughing face to heart eyes with a loud high-pitched giggle.

"Alright, say I'm interested. What kind of art are we talking? Painting? Statue? Digital installation?"

"That's more like it!" Rabbit says, their expression sobbing dramatically. "Nothing you can't handle. Just a painting. One of those really old tactile pieces. 'Girl with a Pearl Earring' from the 15th century or something."

"17th century," I correct automatically, no longer fully in the conversation. I'd written a thesis on that very painting, spent hours fascinated by digital replicas, wondering what the girl in the portrait was thinking, who she had been. Dreaming of what the world had been like when she'd been alive. Very few people know that about me, and I like to keep it that way. But the existence of that particular painting, in the Scitek building, leaves me feeling adrift. Did Derek…? No. I left years ago. There's no way he bought it because of me.

Rabbit raises their hands. "Okay whatever. You know the one then."

"Yeah, I know it." I feel hot and cold at the same time. I'm not sure I'm in my body anymore.

"So you in?" Rabbit asks, and I read tension in the set of their shoulders. We've built a business relationship this last year, but all the jobs they've given me have been mid-level at best. Mostly digital installations, some 21st century tactile pieces. Middling risk, middling payments. This would be a breakthrough for Rabbit, a chance to build a reputation with gold-blood clients and get obscenely rich, a fixer's wet dream. The dual call, the nerves, tell me that it's also a first-time client — which means bigger risk, and I bet Rabbit's desperate to make this happen. Unease coils in my stomach, but the painting has gotten under my skin. I can't let this one go.

"Yeah. What's my upfront?"

Rabbit names a price and goosebumps rise on my arms. It's the kind of money that could turn someone into a gold-blood. It's not even the full payment.

"What's the catch?" I ask.

"They want it in two days."

"No way. I'd need a week at least to prep properly." I'm lying, but it's always better to ask for more time.

Rabbit glitches again and I wait patiently. They stabilize after a few moments. "Three days."

Now it's down to negotiating details. "I want a bonus upfront for that timeline."

Rabbit's hologram pixelates once more, then reforms. "Okay. Client is willing to add a fifteen percent bonus upfront."

"Fine. They have any additional details?"

"The painting is hung in boardroom 112X, there's three central elevators that need an employee chip to operate. Air entrance is on the 50th floor."

Figures. No one with this client's kind of money is going in at dark level. Gold-bloods aren't going to get ground filth on their expensive shoes.

"Alright. Three days. Usual drop-off procedures," I say.

I shut down the link, the light of the comms projection scanner blinking out from the cone around me. I pull the balaclava off my face with a sigh. The sudden return to quiet without the digital noise of the bobblehead's bright sounds is a relief. I shed the parka and sunglasses and shove my hair out of my face. Old school beats AI every time, but the price is overheating.

I spin in my chair and find three incredulous faces looking at me.

"Holy shit," Enix, our biohacker, says. He's massive, bald, and covered in tattoos that he likes to show off by wearing a wife-beater and shorts. Either that or he can't find any other clothes that will fit him. He's sprawled on the beat-up synth-leather couch, taking up two cushions to himself. "Are we seriously doing this, Ro?"

"Yep," I say brightly. "Think of the less shitty apartments we'll all be able to afford after this."

"I've only got rudimentary data on the layout and security protocols for the Scitek building," Ruby says, perched on a stool at the kitchen counter, chewing on a fingernail out of habit. Her dark bangs are nearly hanging in her deep brown eyes, and she's got her trademark red sneaks on. She's our nethacker, and damn good at her job. Whatever keeps her awake at night, she comes by it honestly — one of her legs is entirely cybernetic and I don't think that it's due to a birth defect.

"This feels personal," comments Tor, his black boots propped up on the coffee table from where he's observing us all from the ratty armchair. My counter-AI specialist, and a right pain in the ass. He has an unnerving habit of saying things that punch through all my layers of masks.

He's also irritatingly good looking with a strong jaw and sharp cheekbones — but none of it is modded. The slight imperfections of his skin, the minute asymmetry of his features, they give away that it's all natural. Even the circuit lines at his temples that indicate significant neurological augments somehow add to his appearance. I'd hate him less for it if there'd been an aesthetician involved — vanity would have been a crack in the impenetrable wall of his righteousness.

"With this much money on the line, everything's personal," I snap back, then wince at my loss of cool.

I run a hand through my short hair and sigh. I turn away from Tor, looking to the most rational member of the team. "Ruby, I trust you. You'll figure out a way."

The underworld thinks AgentLOL is a genius lone wolf operative. The reality is that I'm a physical operative with a support team. Nobody with my kind of record works alone.

Ruby doesn't smile, but she straightens a little bit. "I always do."

It's a relief that she's onboard. If she dissents, that's when I know I need to rethink something.

"I'm going to need some entry and exit options, the cleaning and guard contracts and schedules, any extra security protocols, lockdown procedures, everything you can find. Five hours, Ruby," I state.

She nods, her expression resolute. She drops off the kitchen stool and moves to what I fondly think of as our ops wall — it's covered in screens that can show anything from diagnostics to the news. Or Enix's favourite sitcoms when we're not on a job. They're currently all dark. Below them are four net stations, with connection ports and comfy chairs for while we're uploaded. Mine is mostly unused, but Ruby can usually be found linked up. I've never asked what she does with all that time.

Our headquarters was once a lower-level apartment that could be rented without too many questions being asked. Cockroaches are a small price to pay for the complete soundproofing of the building, and the inability to trace it to any of us. It's got a bedroom with an actual bed which is kind of mine, but Tor and Ruby are over so often that we all end up rotating through sleeping on the bed or on one of the two living room couches. The other bedroom has been turned into Enix's lab, and he's got his own extra-long bed to stretch out in there. He's a better roommate than my university ones ever were.

I like our setup. It feels safe.

Ruby sits down at her station and presses open the cybernetics port on her arm, common as breathing air these days. She pulls out wires and plugs into her console, sending her consciousness into the net that permeates North City and ensures that everything keeps running. Her face goes slack as her eyes roll into the back of her head, her consciousness no longer in her body. I hate uploading myself, personally, but to each their own. Living in my own body is bad enough as it is.

There's no point in staring at Ruby while she's out, and I don't want to keep talking to Tor.

"Enix, you had some experimental augments you wanted to show me?"

"Yes ma'am," the big man says and his expression brightens. "They're in the back."

I get up to follow him as he limps away, but give Tor's legs a kick in passing. "No feet on the table."

He scowls at me and slowly puts his boots down on the ground. In mocking imitation, he says, "Yes ma'am."

He can't see it, but I roll my eyes anyways.

* * *

"It's always the subcontractors that are the weak points," Enix comments.

"Supply chain's the easiest attack vector. Doesn't matter how much of a security protocol a place has got if they don't make sure their suppliers are clean," Tor says.

I'm not really interested in hearing them philosophize on the best way to get a job done. I want to get this over with. Hold the painting in my own two hands, for a few moments.

"Alright, I think we've got a plan," I interrupt as we all stand around the hologram projection of the interior of the Scitek HQ hovering over the coffee table.

It glitters green as it rotates slowly in the dim air between us as I look each team member in the eyes.

Ruby nods, worrying at a thumbnail with her teeth. One day I should really get her a stress ball to squeeze instead. Or forcibly paint her nails with capsaicin or something.

Enix grins. "I'm looking forward to this."

His enthusiasm is a soothing balm over my own unease. Tor was right. This does feel personal. That painting… she's special to me. But it's more than that. I know this is a huge risk, but I can't back down. Not if Derek's involved. I never did get closure.

Tor, standing with his arms crossed, is frowning. "This is risky."

"Don't tell me you suddenly care for my well-being, Tor," I say lightly, as if he wasn't reading my mind. "Empathy isn't your vibe."

I'm expecting sarcasm in response, but instead he glowers silently at me. I guess he does care, after all. Explains why he sticks around despite his caustic views on all of our operations. I don't like this revelation, however. It's just distracting.

I clear my throat. "Alright then. Rest up, make sure you eat properly. Twenty-two hundred tomorrow is go time."

Ruby looks at me and nods. "I'll get you a uniform by then."

I don't doubt it in the least.

* * *

When we do jobs, I sometimes forget where biomatter ends and where synthetics and machine begin. I'm sitting on the table in Enix's lab as he's got the wires from my cybernetics port plugged into a diagnostics tool. His face is set in a slight frown as he focuses on booting up my cybernetic enhancements one by one with the care of a pre-flight check. I always feel like I should light up like a Christmas tree, but visually, nothing changes about me.

My arms ache faintly from where Enix installed an experimental augment he's been tinkering with for months. I trust him fully — he would never mod me if he wasn't completely confident that it would work. In this case, I hope I don't have to test this one out on the job though.

I let my mind wander, looking over the haphazard collection of materials in his workspace. There's shelves of spare wires and chips and polymer, neatly organized and labelled, and tools laid out in an organized line on his workbench. Sketches of half-baked ideas are taped to the wall, both for augments and tattoos, and I admire his most recent batch of drawings of the anatomical construction of bird wings.

Another augmentation comes online, and my skin buzzes with static for a moment before settling down. I don't like having most of the augments operational day-to-day, as it's a lot of data to process if I'm cooking dinner or taking a shower. I don't need to know the exact chemical composition of my shampoo just by touching it.

There's a few that I've had so long that I notice their lack more than I notice their presence. Enhanced vision, enhanced hearing, biosign monitoring, discreet commslink — these are standard stuff for pretty much anyone with even a little means, and any underworld operative who isn't a steroid-fuelled thug. Then the neuro data analysis module courtesy of my university days.

There's also the stuff that Enix has installed in me over our years working together. A hormone injector for bursts of adrenaline, dopamine, testosterone, estrogen, endorphins, and only Enix knows what else. That's when you know you're dealing with a professional. Performer, thief, assassin; a lot of different kinds of professionals, I guess.

My favourite mod is my skin-lattice, a polymer subdermal netting covering my torso to protect vital organs against anything from a handgun to a rifle. The first upgrade I chose for myself after Derek. Completely illegal if you're not state security. Great if you think your ex is going to put out a hit on you though.

That's not even mentioning the bionetic skeleton that sits along my limbs and makes me faster and stronger than I have any right to be. I've lost track of what else Enix has developed and installed. The number of times I've been under the knife in his lab, I should be a tapestry of scars, but instead my skin is smooth and unmarked. It makes me uneasy whenever I think about it too long, so I do my best not to. I'm glad Enix has never asked me why I'm made of synth-skin.

Living under the radar works in my favour. I can't be found by anyone I don't want finding me, and the authorities can't bioscreen me. I've got so many illegal mods installed they'd either execute me immediately or forcibly conscript me. Which honestly sounds worse.

Hunting down misguided idealist Union activists as some sort of drugged up super soldier is not exactly how I want to spend my days. Not that this life is one I planned for either. I wanted to be a gallery curator, spend my days surrounded by art. Instead, Enix's tattoo collection is as close as I get to that dead dream, these days.

Enix finishes his diagnostics tests and says, "Alright, everything's playing nice together."

"Excellent," I say. "Let's keep it that way."

"One of these days I should really figure out that chip in your neck," Enix comments. "It hasn't interfered yet, but it's weird tech and I don't like not knowing what it does."

I touch my free hand to it instinctively. A memory of excruciating pain flares up momentarily before fading away. Something must read on my face, as Enix raises an eyebrow. "Or not?"

"Maybe just remove it," I say as calmly as I can.

Enix rubs the back of his neck thoughtfully. "It's a tricky spot, really easy to nick your artery. But yeah, sure, we can do that."

I force a smile. I don't like thinking about the chip. Or most of my body for that matter.

Ruby's already plugged into the net, and I experience her as a disembodied voice in my head. "Comms check."

"I hear you loud and clear," I say out loud.

"Great," she says. "The sooner this is over the better."

Tor, also plugged into the net, grumbles in my mind. "This is a bad idea, Ro."

"You say that every time," I say breezily.

"I mean it this time." His deep voice resonates in my head.

"Well, it's happening anyways, so let's all make sure it goes smoothly." I have an edge in my voice and a line of tension between my shoulders.

Enix disconnects his comms for a second to say, "Tor seriously needs to get laid."

I snort, but my shoulders drop. "Yeah, seriously. He's wound way too tight."

"Are you talking about me?" Tor asks.

"Nah, some other guy me and Enix know," I reply sweetly, then make an exasperated face at Enix.

The large man chuckles and disconnects the wires from the cybernetics port on my arm and closes it with the flap of synth-skin. Still off comms as he packages up his diagnostics tool, he quietly says, "Good luck Ro. I'll be monitoring your biosigns. Shout if you need anything."

I slide off the table and loop my arms around him in a hug, my arms barely wrapping the width of his chest. I don't normally like touching people like this anymore, but Enix has always felt like safety to me. He was the one who found me when I ran from my old life, and introduced me to my new line of work. I owe him. He's also one of the few people who looks at me as a person, and not only this body that I didn't ask for.

He hugs back gently, afraid of his own strength. He's the result of a failed genetics experiment to make super soldiers, leaving him with lopsided limbs and no official documentation to prove his existence. His choices were to either work in the underworld and actually use his brilliant mind, or be a menial labourer in the dark level barely scraping by. Everything in this city runs on official identification if you want to be someone. It's shit.

When we disengage, Enix limps away to take up his station in the main room. I trail after him and survey the room. Ruby and Tor's faces are both slack as if sleeping, sprawled in their respective reclining chairs. It's tempting to sharpie something rude onto Tor's forehead for when he wakes up, but that would be childish even for me.

With a final nod to myself, I shrug out of my favourite black jacket that I've sewn neon patches onto over the years, pull on a cleaner's shapeless grey jumpsuit and a dark wig, and check its placement in the bathroom mirror. I don't know how Ruby managed to get a Nuvo Cleaning uniform delivered to our door on such short notice, but I'm quite certain her network of contacts would make state security weep with envy.

My face is wan and drawn under the chin-length wig with blunt bangs, but it does a good job of disguising the true shape of my face, as well as some of the traces of cybernetics on my scalp. I look like someone else, and it unsettles me more than my reflection normally does. The jumpsuit, at least, has the benefit of disguising the true lines of my body, and it feels like a kind of armour. It makes me unremarkable.

I turn away and start walking. It's show time.

PART
TWO

Down at the dark level, the air is perpetually humid and too warm for comfort. In old times this might have been called street level, but now it's a dim twilight zone lit only by blinding digital advertisements for everything from dental implants to sex shows several floors above. It also smells terribly of stagnant water, mold, rot, garbage, and shit. Anyone who can afford to avoid coming down here, does.

This is where the city's poorest exist, never seeing the sky, boxed in by the cage of all the skyscrapers and pedestrian bridges and platforms that form the working corridors of the city several storeys up. If you don't officially exist, you can't work, or you don't want to be found, this is where you end up. Rock bottom, as the saying goes. Unless you're crazy enough to join the Union, who think they can somehow fix our broken system. A complete waste of time, if you ask me.

The Scitek building is an oddity in the city. It doesn't connect at the working levels - either you come in by air, or at the dark level. It's the tallest building in the city, a monolith with a clear space around it that only emphasizes its height. The state apparatus that claims to be our government could only dream of having a building this shining, this clean. You know where true power is in North City by how maintained a building is.

I take the normal pedestrian trams and passageways several floors above dark level, the beating heart of North City. There's nothing remarkable about me in this disguise as a cleaner; just another person with a job to do. No one looks at me twice, which is exactly how I want this to go. I still pick the routes with the least cameras though, just in case. I dread the day that bioscanners get installed everywhere — I won't be able to go out, then. The city's corporate overlords are pushing for them though, for "security". More like control. As if we aren't all already scrutinized to within an inch of our lives.

I try to make myself as small as possible — I hate being touched, and the press of strangers in confined spaces makes me extra tense. I focus on running through all of the information from Ruby's briefing on the guard schedules, reciting them silently like a meditation.

It's late enough in the evening that there are youths in party outfits on the trams, clearly already drunk or a little bit high. It's a weekday, but who's going to blame them for wanting to take the edge off their existence? Tomorrow will come sooner than anyone wants.

They're loud though, and I itch to have space to myself again. When I step off my last tram, it's a relief to be able to move freely.

The descent to the dark level is on staircases with rusted handrails and crumbling concrete, sharp-eyed people staring at me suspiciously from their patchwork tents or box homes. It's tempting to check my reflexes for the blade in my arm in case of danger, but I keep the irrational impulse in check. I don't need to draw attention to myself. Just keep walking.

When I'm down in the dripping damp, unknowable substances squelching under my boots, I make sure to stick to the shadows. I might be modded into something approximating a soldier if you squint hard enough, but it still isn't safe. I don't need some crystal-fueled maniac trying to grab my stuff. Not that I have anything worth stealing on me at the moment, if you ignore my actual physical self. I've heard ugly rumours of black markets for stolen cybernetics, ripped out of unwilling victims while they're awake. Not a fate I'm hoping for tonight.

There's more tents and boxes and blankets lining the streets amongst the occasional street vendor who's selling what I suspect is roasted rat or other delicacies only found down here. They call out, hawking their excellent prices, but I keep my eyes on the path directly ahead of me. It's an uncomfortable reminder of where I might have ended up, had Enix not found me sobbing and hysterical in a surgical gown and taken pity on me.

As I get close to the Scitek building, I look up briefly, unable to see the top of the HQ. Sparkling windows stretch up as far as I can see. I know from Ruby's stolen data that all employees live in the lower levels, and there's even a company store, school, and entertainment level so there's no reason to leave, ever. Another day of work to get another day deeper in debt. Great for security if your people never leave. Nobody's going to be selling secrets to competitors if they can't actually get out.

The middle levels are all the labs and general offices. I don't give a shit about those. As I told Rabbit, I don't do corporate espionage.

I shuffle to the dark level entrance, a blast-resistant metal double door, and note the two guards flanking it. There are also automatic turrets, currently dormant, installed above the door. I know from Ruby's briefing that the guards can activate them in under five seconds, and if a guard dies, the turrets turn on automatically. I'm not sure why Scitek is prepared to be sieged, but I'm hoping to avoid getting riddled with bullet holes today.

I've got a duffel of old clothes in hand and a doctored photo of a younger me with parents that aren't mine. Just enough to look like I'm moving in to work as a new cleaner. It also helps that my face looks perpetually young and vulnerable, despite the fact that I'm almost thirty. Most people aren't too suspicious of me.

As I look over the guards, both wearing bulky external armour with digital visors hiding the top half of their faces, Ruby comments, "They're wearing old model X-22s. Bullet and flame proof, increases soldier's carry capacity two times over. Too bulky though, the new X-30s allow faster movement."

I don't react to the information, but Ruby's got way more info about military technology specs than a civilian should. I am absolutely convinced that she also used to be state security, not that she would ever admit it. I tried asking her about it once, and it made her so mad that she screamed at me that I was a nosey bitch. Which coming from her, was so terrifying I never brought it up again. I also gave her apology chocolates — the good kind, not the cheap synth shit.

The left guard, a woman with pale skin, her chest plate clearly labelled Scitek Security - no subcontractors here — has her hands casually holding her fully-automatic assault rifle across her chest as she gives me a once over. I'm wearing the official uniform of Nuvo Cleaning, the subcontractor Scitek uses. She glances at her partner, a man with dark skin, who doesn't even bother to look at me, his gaze roaming the street.

"Hello," I say, making my voice meek. "I was told to report here for work?"

The guard sighs. "Paperwork and identification."

She holds out a digital scanner, and I press the ID chip in

my wrist against it. Enix programmed an entire life's worth of history into it, with assistance from Ruby who got into Nuvo's systems to make sure all the administration was perfect in every detail. My real ID chip is sitting in a plastic case back in Enix's lab.

I can see the file flicker into existence on her digital visor, and I watch her eyes rapidly move from side to side as she reads. I can feel a bead of sweat trickling down my back. It is far too warm down here. After a few moments of tense silence, she closes the file and her visor returns to neutral. "Alright, everything checks out. Report to office 1C for programming to gain access to your apartment and assigned cleaning floors."

I smile nervously and say, "Thank you."

The guard swipes the lock panel and opens the door to usher me into a blank white hallway. As soon as the door clicks shut behind me, air filters kick on and suck the humidity back out. I stand still for a moment, squinting as if my eyes need to adjust to the new, warm lighting. No cleaner could afford the mods I've got.

When I judge the ruse is complete, I move down the corridor to 1C, and find a bored man flicking through vids on a screen over his desk.

I knock on the open door and timidly half-step into the office. "Um, hello?"

He glances up and his mouth tightens in annoyance. "Who're you?"

"I was hired by Nuvo to clean? The guard outside said I should see you for programming."

"Alright, fine. What's your name?"

"Alice Shad."

He frowns and consults a database. "Let's see, Alice, yes. Room 5H, single, no dependents. Alright, hold out your arm.

You'll have access to floors 1 through 110. The top floors are restricted. Special permissions are needed for those."

I already know this, but I nod along anyways.

Tentatively, I hold out my arm without the identifier chip, and he takes out a large gauge syringe and says, "This will hurt."

I look at him with big eyes but stay mute.

He isn't gentle as he jabs the needle into my arm and injects a microchip. I make a soft sound of pain and let tears well up in my eyes as he retracts the syringe and carelessly puts a bandage over the site. It's not needed, as I have increased healing factor augments, but he doesn't know that. I also don't want him to notice that my arm is synth-skin.

The man looks unimpressed as I hold my arm to my chest. I want him to remember just another mousey, uninteresting menial labourer.

"Elevators are down the hall, can't miss them. Every floor has a janitorial closet by the elevators, clearly marked. You're on the night shift so you're already late. Put your things away and get started immediately. Shift lead is Martin, he'll be on the 75th floor and can tell you which floors are yours. The Scitek orientation and welcome video is pre-loaded in your room. Watch it at the end of your shift."

I bob my head, doing my best to look nervous. "Okay, thank you."

"Yeah," he says dismissively, his eyes already back on his vids.

I scurry away to the elevator, maintaining my charade. As instructed, I deposit my bag of belongings in the spartan studio apartment assigned to Alice Shad. The apartment is no more than a narrow bed, kitchen, and bathroom. Function over comfort, I guess. I pause to reset the photoframe to its default landscape of a beach and ocean, a sight only the rich can afford to see in reality. A fact that fills me with a deep sense of shame. But, no need to leave evidence of my real face lying around.

"Comms check," I say.

"Good," Ruby chirps.

"Here," Tor says.

"Vitals are steady," Enix reports.

"I'm heading up now," I say.

"I'm masking your face in the vidfeeds," Tor adds. "For such a security-conscious company, their AI for facial recognition is several versions out of date."

"Good," I answer, and take a moment to roll out my shoulders before hunching back into my persona of a timid new cleaner. I leave the room and shuffle back to the elevators.

The ride to the 75th floor is long, but the elevator moves so smoothly I lose all sense of motion. There's a screen on one wall playing more advertisements, this time for new items at the company store. They're all over-priced, but for the convenience of not having to either pay for air transport or trudge through the dark level, I bet most Scitek employees buy them anyways. I keep my head down with my hands clasped in front of me in case anyone should join my ride, but thankfully, no one does.

Eventually, the elevator dings and the doors slide open with a soft woosh of air. There's a guard leaning against the opposite wall, who eyes me dubiously and straightens up as I step into the hallway. He's got a lined face and greying hair, and I would bet good money he's previously served in state security. Something about the straightness to his spine. He doesn't have the same heavy armour as the guards outside, instead wearing a dark blue uniform with the Scitek logo stitched on the left breast, but his assault rifle is just as impeccably well-maintained.

He straightens up and asks, "Who are you?"

I ring my hands. "It's my first day, I'm looking for Martin. My name is Alice."

The guard gestures for my arm, and I hold out the freshly-bandaged microchip. He scans it, then sighs. "Nuvo really needs to get its shit together. They keep sending us cleaners in the middle of shifts. Martin's inside, shouldn't be hard to find."

Thank you, Ruby, for finding that flaw in Nuvo's scheduling. Bureaucratic incompetence creates weaknesses to exploit.

"Okay, thank you. Sorry."

"Not your fault," the guard says and resumes leaning against the wall. "Welcome to the Scitek building."

I smile tentatively before I push open the door that leads into the offices. I step into a hallway that's lined with paintings, but I know that they're not mere décor. Ruby's brief included details on the security features of this place, which includes hidden turrets built into the painting frames. God help anyone stupid enough to try to use force in this building.

Or stupid enough to get caught somewhere where they shouldn't be. Nerves jitter in my chest, but I ignore them.

"Ruby, anything?"

I know she has alternate optical feeds from my visual augments, one of which is heat signatures. I hate having that many visuals layered over top of reality, so I feed them back to base.

"Looks like three heat signatures at desks, and one person moving about."

"Martin, the head cleaner. Guide me."

I start down the hallway, a prickle at the base of my neck giving me the feeling of being watched, but I know it's only my own awareness of walking through danger. My steps eventually lead me to an intersection, and Ruby instructs me to turn right. I follow, casually glancing in through the windowed doors of offices and labs, but don't see anything out of place.

Eventually Ruby says, "Heat signature at desk on your left up ahead."

I slow my steps and take a quick peek inside — it's a young man passed out on top of his keyboard. That's a relief. Not sure why he didn't take the elevator down to his apartment, though. It's not like it's a long commute. Must have fallen asleep by accident.

I tiptoe past him, and ask, "How far?"

"You're close, just a little farther."

I cross another intersection and head straight through as instructed.

"Hey!"

I freeze and turn towards the sound. It's a different employee, also male, but older. He waves at me impatiently to come closer from the door of his office, down one of the hallways I don't want to take. Under my breath I mutter, "Someone's awake."

"Tracking," Tor says.

I get to the employee who is a little bit taller than me with a receding hairline and heavy brows that are knitted into a scowl. "You're not the usual cleaner."

I keep my eyes low. "I'm Alice."

"The coffee machine is clogged with grounds again. I don't know how I'm expected to meet deadlines if I can't even have my coffee. Fix it now."

Ugh. "Sorry sir, right away. Can you point me to the machine…?"

He sighs heavily as if I've asked the most asinine question in the world. "I don't understand how it's so hard to find competent cleaners. There are enough people clamouring for any job at all that you'd think we'd have better help."

I don't say anything and keep my eyes down. Inside, I'm seething. I'm familiar with the type of asshole who gets off on having on their boot on someone else's neck.

Not getting a reaction, he points towards what I assume is a kitchenette and says, "Over there. Make it quick."

"Okay sir," I reply, and follow his direction. One of the doors opens into a small kitchenette, and before I step in, I glance over my shoulder.

The employee is still standing, watching me with his arms crossed. I guess I really am cleaning a coffee machine tonight. That's a new one. Fuck.

It's a standard machine and seems to be the same kind that we keep in our headquarters. I know it has a nasty habit of malfunctioning if the grounds aren't emptied. Sure enough, when I open it up, there's several cups' worth of coffee grinds that haven't been emptied. I roll my eyes to myself that no one bothered to actually empty it out after they used it. Coffee is one of the biggest luxury items in North City, as only a few portions of the planet can still support growing plantations. Everyone else has to get by with stimpacks, which are probably more effective, but aren't the same experience at all.

"What are you doing?" Ruby asks.

"Cleaning a coffee machine," I mutter under my breath.

"Can you do the one in here next?" Enix asks.

"Very funny," I say through gritted teeth. I hear Tor snort, and Enix laughs. I ignore them.

Coffee is the only luxury I haven't been able to let go of. Probably because it's delicious… and addictive.

It takes me a few minutes to scrub out the machine, and I try not to let my impatience get the best of me. I need to keep this cover, and as much as I'd love to sucker punch the employee, there's bigger things at stake tonight. I click the coffee machine closed, and step back out into the hallway.

The man is still standing, waiting impatiently. I don't really want to get closer to him, but he's also in my way. I shuffle closer and clasp my hands in front of me. When I'm near enough that I can speak softly, I say, "It should work now."

"Good," he says in a tone that implies I'm still a disappointment, before he steps back into his office to retrieve a mug. I take the opportunity to slip away down the hallway I actually want.

"Cleared," I whisper.

"Target is just up ahead," Ruby says.

She's right, he's pushing a cleaning cart down the hallway from one office to the next.

The floor is carpeted, so my footfalls are too soft for him to hear me approach.

Martin, the head cleaner, turns out to be a stocky man a few inches shorter than me, with thick dark hair shot through with grey.

When I say hello, he jumps and backs a step away. It takes him a moment to register my uniform, and when he does, he frowns deeply, his dark brows forming a straight line across his face.

"You're new. Who're you?"

"Alice Shad, I started today. I was told to report to you?"

Martin doesn't stop frowning. "I don't remember any new cleaners starting today."

I shrug, and clasp my hands in front of me. "This is what I was told."

He sighs heavily and rubs a hand across his face. "There's a training protocol we're supposed to follow, but since you're here, I guess you can shadow me."

"Video feed is looping for the next two minutes," Tor says.

"A guard patrol will be coming through in ten," Ruby reminds me.

I move like physics don't apply to me. One moment Martin is standing looking at me, the next I have him in a headlock, my arms perfectly aligned to pinch off the blood flow to his brain. He's so startled that he doesn't make a sound for a moment, enough time for me to clamp my other hand over his mouth and begin dragging him into the nearest office.

His legs are kicking and he desperately claws at my arms, but in less than a minute, he goes limp in my arms. I count to ten before gently lowering him to the ground with a whispered apology, and use a rag from the cleaning cart to gag him. I pull plastic cuffs from my pocket and attach his hands to the desk, then cuff his ankles together. I pause for a moment, listening. There are no approaching footsteps. Good.

I open the cybernetics panel on his arm and plug myself directly into it. "Alright, go."

"On it," Enix says.

I wait, straining my ears for sounds of people approaching, my mouth dry.

Finally, Enix says, "Done. Your new microchip is coded like his. You'll have access to the top levels now, but the stair accesses will need Tor's help."

I breathe out deeply. "Good."

We already knew about the extra security on the stair doors, so no surprises yet.

I know Martin will wake up shortly, and I need to be gone before then. I pull his cart into the small office, close the blinds on the window looking out into the hallway, and grab a broom and dustbin before stepping out and pulling the door shut behind me.

I begin walking down the hallway and ask, "Where next?"

Ruby says, "There's an emergency staircase at the end of the hall."

"Will I have access?"

"Yes. It's the upper levels that will need Tor's assistance."

"Perfect," I respond, and keep walking.

I hope Martin doesn't get fired. Maybe I'll need to have Ruby put some of my earnings into his account after this if he does. I don't know if he has family, but I'd hate for them to go hungry because of me.

The emergency staircase is well marked, and doesn't even need me to swipe to open. When the door swings shut behind me with a click, I pause for a moment and scan both up and down. I don't hear anyone else in here with me.

"Ruby?"

"Clear."

The concrete stairs are entirely closed in, with digital screens on one wall cycling through ads which I can easily ignore. Instead, I turn my gaze towards my goal, and start moving upwards, two steps at a time.

* * *

3 7 floors later, I'm a little out of breath and my thigh muscles are warm, but I've barely broken a sweat. Pre-modding, I probably would have been crying on the ground twenty floors ago. Despite that, I still miss what I used to be. The softness that used to be mine.

I'm standing in front of a metal door labelled "112" and "Restricted Area".

"Alright, ready?" I ask, eyeing the chip reader next to the door.

I know that if this goes wrong, I'm going to be incinerated by the flamethrower hanging menacingly over the door, as if the warning on the door wasn't already cause for concern.

"Yeah," Tor says. "I'm going to need you to hold your arm to the reader until I tell you to remove it, as still as you can."

"Okay." I take a deep breath to steady myself. The plastic of the chip reader is cool when my arm makes contact, and I hold it perfectly still. Another perk of modification — preternatural stillness. In spite of this, I close my eyes, bracing for the lick of flames to consume me.

Seconds crawl by.

There's a cheery beep.

"You're clear," Tor says.

I pull open the door before the system can change its mind and quickly step through. I don't relax until it's completely shut behind me. "Thanks."

"It's why I'm here," Tor replies.

I shake my head but look around.

"Ruby?"

"A few faint heat signatures, other end of the floor. Shouldn't be a problem."

"Great. Lead on."

Ruby provides crisp instructions in my head, and I follow them until I'm standing in front of the genuine wood door labelled "112X".

I try the handle and find it won't budge, but there's a chip reader.

"I'm scanning the chip again," I comment.

"This one shouldn't need me according to Ruby's network topology," Tor says, "but I'm on standby."

Not entirely comforting.

I scan my chip, and the reader beeps in acceptance. I push open the boardroom door and step in, letting it swing shut behind me. I'm immediately struck by the opposite wall — it's entirely made of windows. From Ruby's briefing I know that these are true windows facing the outside, not digital screens. They're also shatter, bullet, blast, and cut resistant.

For a moment, I forget why I'm here. Transfixed by a view I haven't seen in years, I lean my broom and dustpan against the wall and step closer to the windows and look out at the glittering lights of North City spread out below me. It's hard to pick out specific buildings, it's just an abstract landscape of dark shadows, bright windows and moving digital ads. The buildings are clustered so densely together that it's impossible to see the edge of the city where the barrier wall is. I'm up high enough, however, that I can also see the dark expanse of the sky. I squint faintly, trying to cancel out the lights of the city to better see the faint pale specks of a handful of stars. "It's beautiful," I breathe.

"The painting?" Tor asks, confused.

His voice in my head annoys me, but it also brings me back to reality. "No, the sky."

"Not the time for stargazing, Ro," Tor says.

"Is there ever a time?" I comment.

I'm not expecting an answer and I don't get one.

I remember parties on rooftops where the sky was such a common sight that no one paid it any mind. If I could go back, I would ignore all the glittering gold-bloods and their drama and just sit and watch the night sky. Why did I not do it when I had the chance? Did I think that the view would never be denied to me?

Before the seas rose and the equatorial belt became an uninhabitable wasteland, I knew the sky had been a common good. Yet now, with humanity forced polewards into artificial cities owned and run by corporate greed, the sky is a precious treasure reserved only for the wealthy. Who don't bother to appreciate it.

Anger flares for a moment, and Enix asks, "I'm seeing a cortisol spike. Everything alright?"

"Yeah, sorry," I say. "Just thinking about how unfair everything is."

"Need a dopamine boost?" he asks.

"No, I'm good. Give it a minute and I'll be fine."

"Roger," he replies.

I turn from the windows and survey the room. The center is

held by a heavy, real wooden table with thickly padded chairs circling it. The walls are panelled with more pale wood, and I wonder how much just this room had cost to furnish. The thought is distracting, however, and my eyes move to land on the small painting of an unknown girl with her hair wrapped in blue and yellow cloth, a single heavy white pearl dangling from her ear. The pigments are vibrant, even after centuries of time. Her face is luminous.

I approach and study her for a moment. It always struck me that she looks surprised, or perhaps on the point of speaking, as if someone had intruded on a private moment. Which is impossible, considering that to make a textile art piece like this it would have taken numerous hours of work and would have been carefully planned. With my augmented vision, I can make out details I hadn't seen before: her eyelashes are faintly visible, and I pick out the sweep of a green curtain in the backdrop that hadn't been present in the digital recreations. Secrets to the naked eye.

No one has time to make art like this anymore. Its all fast, consumable digital work churned out by AI algorithms to suit an individual's exact preferences. There's no need to invest in mastery when the net will provide you with exactly what you want in only a few seconds.

Maybe that's why I studied the history of tactile art. To remember that things used to be different. That people used to be able to make art. A useless pursuit, as my parents kept saying at the time. Looking at Vermeer's "Girl with the Pearl Earring", I wonder if they were right. It's only gold-bloods who get to see old art like this, now. Whatever survived in the chaos of the climactic transition, anyways.

If I hadn't spent years in hiding, it would be tempting to vidcall my parents now and tell them that I should have listened to them. It would have saved me a lot of grief, even if it wasn't for the reasons they thought.

I shake my head to clear it and study the frame. As I anticipated, there are sensors hidden within it, monitoring for any movement. There's also a small port hidden in the bottom of the gold filigreed frame, and I carefully jack into it, careful not to move the frame even a millimetre. My augments allow me that level of precision.

"Ruby, do your thing."

I wait silently as she turns off the sensors on the frame while still sending the expected signals back to the security centre so no alarms are raised.

"You're good," Ruby finally says.

"Thanks," I say and unplug myself before carefully removing the painting from the wall. It's quite a small piece, conveniently for me. "Any sign of people approaching?"

"Cameras are clear," Tor says.

"No heat signatures or auditory anomalies on your sensor suite," Ruby adds. "Guard patrol is scheduled for this floor in five minutes."

"Good," I say distractedly as I carefully remove the frame from the painting. When done, I return the frame to the wall, now hanging empty.

I pull on a pair of white cotton gloves from my pocket and very carefully begin removing the painting from its internal frame so that it is a flat piece of canvas. I am conscious of the fragility of this work, and take care not to damage the several centuries old material. It seems almost comical — I had spent months thinking about this very painting to earn my degree, and now here I am, touching it, risking its very existence.

I take out a flexi-protector from my pocket and split it into its four components, placing each one at a corner of the canvas. When they're in place, I activate the protector, watching as the faint blue mesh glows into existence, preserving the canvas in its exact state at this moment. Confident now that I'm not going to harm this painting, I delicately roll it up. When I slip it into the thin tube I have smuggled against my lower back, everything about this job seems absurd.

Who had come into this place and seen this painting, here in this boardroom, and wanted it so badly they hired a mid-level underworld fixer to get it for them? Had I met them at one of those extravagant parties in the past?

It might have been simpler for the client to simply offer to buy it. But then again, maybe the owner had refused to part with it.

The owner.

My nerve endings prickle with unease.

I slip the tube back against my lower back and rezip my uniform to hide it from sight. The tube is temperature and humidity-controlled, so I'm not worried about the painting getting wrecked even if this mission goes south.

As I step towards the door, I freeze with the sudden, overpowering urge to know whether or not Derek had done it for me. If the painting was because of me.

"Ruby, where are the nearest stairs?"

"That's not the plan, Ro," Tor replies instead. "We agreed on elevators to the 50th floor and out through the air entrance."

"I'm changing the plan," I say. "I need to check something."

"There are several emergency stairs, the nearest is out the door and to the right," Ruby says. "But Tor is right. We should stick to the plan."

"Listen, I've got the objective, everything's gone smoothly. I just want to make a small detour."

"I don't like it," Enix adds. "Your heartbeat is elevated."

I blow out a breath of frustration. "Please, everyone. Help me do this."

"I told you this felt personal," Tor says. Damn him. "You're letting your history cloud your judgement."

I wish I had never let it slip that I'd dated someone important at Scitek. Dated. Been engaged to. Was horribly betrayed by. I'm glad the others don't know anything past that. Or who he is.

Anger flares up brightly. "I'm doing this no matter what any of you say. So, you can either help or you can shut the fuck up."

Glorious silence fills my mind as I walk out of the boardroom and head to the right as Ruby directed, broom and dustpan back in hand.

Finally, Enix says, "We'll help."

"Good," I snap, then feel calmness wash over me. That is courtesy of Enix flooding my system with hormones, guaranteed. Now relaxed, I add, "Thank you."

"No problem," Enix replies.

They must have debated helping me amongst themselves. I'm glad they saw the sense in working with me. I'm the one taking all the risks in person, after all.

"Guard patrol is on this floor. It looks like they're starting on the opposite corner from you," Ruby informs me.

"Okay. Plenty of time then."

Ruby guides me to the nearest stairs, a different set from the ones I took to this floor, and I check for a chip reader. There's none, and I can only suppose that's a safety feature. Works for me. I step into the stairwell, ignoring the flashing advertisements, and take the stairs two at a time. I climb up the last three storeys to the very top floor, to yet another door marked "Restricted Access".

I pause at the topmost landing and turn on the spot. "Ruby?"

"No heat signatures," she says. "No auditory anomalies."

"Perfect," I say. "Tor, another chip reader."

"You should turn around while you still can," he says.

"No. You either help, or you live with me turning into fire-roasted kebab."

I hear him sigh heavily. "You're a stubborn idiot, but fine. Hold your arm out."

I hold my wrist to the chip reader, swallowing hard against the nervous lump in my throat, hoping that I won't be rendered to ash along with my favourite painting.

The reader beeps and Tor says, "You're clear."

I pull open the door and step through. "It'll just take a minute, I promise."

PART THREE

The door clicks shut behind me and I stop to look around. I'm no longer in a maze of hallways but an open space. There are various plants here, and each desk has way more space. The air smells fresh in a way that most places don't. Despite having been romantically involved with Scitek's biggest asshole, I've never been to this building. I never wanted to, mind you. Office buildings aren't exactly great date locations.

I take another step forward, and the cool sensation of a bioscan reading me washes over me, and I realize that I have seriously fucked up. This wasn't part of Ruby's briefing. It shouldn't have been there. I lunge towards the door to the stairs, but I only tug on the handle ineffectively — it's already locked. An alarm begins blaring.

"Oh shit."

"Ro, you need to get out of there, lockdown procedure is initiated," Tor says.

"Ruby, options?"

"All staircases and elevators are inaccessible during lockdown. There is a private air pad on this level. You might be able to find a way onto it."

"Can you detect any open windows?" I ask, heart thrumming in my chest.

"I'm trying to stay in their systems, but the lockdown AI is a different beast, I'm really struggling to keep our access," Tor says, sounding like his teeth are gritted in concentration.

"Sorry Ro, with the system instability, I can't get a good reading. You'll have to check yourself visually," Ruby says, her voice quavering.

"That's okay," I say, more trying to reassure myself than anyone else. "I got this."

I drop the stupid broom because there's no point in my disguise anymore and take up a jog, frantically opening doors to peer into boardrooms and offices on the exterior edge of the building. I know this floor is where all the senior executives have their offices, with their support staff in small cubicle farms in the centre of the floor. I don't know how long I have until the guards have marshalled a squad to hunt me down, but I know it won't be long.

There's more art here, I notice distractedly. Marble statues, oil paintings, bronze antiquities. A wealth of human history and artistry, hoarded for a select few to view.

Thankfully, none of them are hiding turrets. Guess the executives are too valuable to accidentally shoot.

I can't think about that now. Focus, Ro.

I finally come to the door marked "CEO" and step in, knowing instinctually that this is where I will find the exit to the private air pad.

It's true, I can see the exit and the rooftop garden and air pad.

But something else catches my attention.

The nameplate on the desk — an old brass thing, a ridiculous anachronism in the otherwise sleek modern office. It reads Derek Long.

Derek.

An image of his face comes unbidden to my mind: tanned skin, dark eyes, the easy smile and always slightly disheveled hair, as if he had just run his fingers through it.

So, he was CEO now. I shouldn't have blocked news feeds about Scitek for so long. His father's retirement and the transition would have made business headlines. Serves me right, I guess, for trying to block everything out about him.

I know I should keep moving and get out while I still can, but I need to know. Why did he get this specific painting? Was it because of me?

I connect to the port in his desk and say, "I need you to bypass the security on the system I just networked to."

"We're barely able to keep access to the broader system," Ruby says, her voice strained. "I can't divide attention."

"We're going to lose access in a few minutes," Tor adds, and I can feel the stress radiating off of him, purely based on tone. "We're risking cybertermination."

Cybertermination. Always a risk for anyone porting their consciousness into the net — if they stay too long, or get attacked by an AI, their consciousness will be erased, leaving only a husk of a physical body behind.

"Get out before that happens," I say. "I'll take it from here."

I take a deep breath and start running through password guesses for Derek's system. Eventually, I hit the right one — his mother's name. Ugh. Typical. That frigid bitch always hated me for, in her words, "stealing her son from her". She always came across as a little bit creepy.

Derek's system opens up to me, and I get my data analytic processor to search his system for the keyword 'Vermeer'.

It takes a few seconds while I shift from foot to foot impatiently, heartbeat thrumming in my ears, until it returns a singular result of a holovid recording.

My heart pounding in my ears, I hit play.

A hologram of Derek appears, casually leaning back in his desk chair, talking to someone I can't see.

> *"Yeah, I'm buying a Vermeer to hang up."*
>
> *"You have a fondness for oil paintings?" the other voice asks.*
>
> *"No. Someone I used to know was very invested in this particular painting, and I want to own it, so that she will never get to lay eyes on the original work."*
>
> *"That's a lot of money to spend out of spite."*
>
> *Derek laughs. "It's barely any money. I'd spend a lot more than this out of spite."*

I shiver. The menace that laces his voice, despite his light tone, is familiar to me. I remember him using that voice on me, warning me of the consequences of not following his exact instructions. I shut the recording off before I have to hear any more. I quickly disconnect myself, feeling dirty from having touched his things, as if his existence might rub off on me.

I can't believe he bought the painting because of me. To spite me. Even though I left him years ago.

A chill settles along my spine. I shouldn't have come here.

I need to run.

Now.

I try the door, but it's locked. I try scanning my chip, but the reader only beeps angrily at me. Surveying the room, there's a heavy paperweight on the desk that looks like some sort of abstract art piece. I heft it in my hand, and figure it's good enough. With one smooth motion, I smash it into the chip reader repeatedly until it crumbles to the floor in pieces. There are wires sticking out from the wall, and I try the door. Still locked. Fuck.

With no better ideas, I connect the wires to my arm, and run my data analytic processor through various impulse patterns until finally the door beeps and I can wrench it towards me with my other hand and keep it wedged open with my foot while I unwire myself. It's such a relief that it actually worked that I feel like I could cry. No time for that though.

Once outside, I drop into a crouch, observing the terrace that I find myself on. There are various topiaries and small shrubs here surrounding the flat open space for landing air transports.

Staying low, I move so that I'm hidden from the windows by some bushes. I know, logically, that the guards probably also have heat sensing visuals so there's no point to it, but the attempt still makes me feel a little bit better.

"I'm outside. How are we all doing?" I whisper.

Now that I'm paying attention, I hear a steady background murmur of faint garbled sounds in my mind.

"Ruby? Tor? Enix?"

Enix responds. "I think I need to forcibly unplug them. They're bleeding from their ears and noses. I can't tell what's happening. They haven't responded in too long."

"NO," Tor shouts at this, and then there's a long silence.

I wait, fretting.

I need my team. I can't lose them. Even Tor and his stupid face.

Gravel grinds together loudly under my feet as I shift my weight.

Ruby, her voice faint and exhausted, says, "We're out of the Scitek networks. We won't be able to get back in."

"We're safe," Tor adds, his voice equally strained.

I breathe out. "Okay. I'm by the airpad. I'm outside."

"We've got an autopilot transport on route. ETA is approximately five minutes," Ruby says. "Can you hold your position?"

"Yeup," I say, scanning my surroundings. "I'm good here."

We go silent for a few moments, until I hear a faint thrumming sound.

"What is that?" I ask. "Is that for me?"

"Shit shit shit," Tor panics. "It's a privately-registered air car. How did we miss this?"

"It only beacons periodically. That's not legal," Ruby adds.

My stomach sinks. There's only one person I know who'd flaunt his disregard for the rules quite so blatantly.

My every instinct screams at me to run. But there's nowhere for me to go. I can't go back inside — I'll just end up target practice for some motivated Scitek guards hoping for a good year-end bonus.

The air car, a sleek all-black thing that barely makes a sound as it pops up over the edge of the building, lands softly in front of me. The driver door raises up, and out steps Derek, dressed in an impeccably-tailored grey suit. He's alone.

He looks directly at me and cocks his head to the side. "Hello Ramona. You've changed your hair."

There's no point in staying down anymore. I stand up. "Fuck you, Derek."

"Tsk, you've forgotten your manners since you started associating with trash."

"You mean stopped associating with trash. The only trash I see in this city is you," I spit back.

He smiles coldly. "What a reunion this is. Come now, you can take off your disguise. There's no need to pretend with me."

I hesitate before deciding I just need to buy time until my ride gets here. I shed the cleaning uniform and carefully pull off my wig. The night air is cool against my skin this high up as I stand in my t-shirt and cargo pants. I make sure to keep my front to him so he can't see the painting tube against my lower back.

Derek walks closer, his hands behind his back. "Well, now

that's more like it. I must say though, Ramona, I hate what you've done with your hair."

I almost reach up to my scalp out of instinct, but I force myself to stillness. I keep most of my hair shaved, with only a small patch of short hair along the crest of my head, which I cycle through different neon-coloured dyes. Currently, a vibrant blue. "I don't care what you like."

He's close enough now that I could reach out and strangle him. The thought is tempting. Derek had always been handsome, but I realize looking at him now that he's been modified — his features are too symmetrical, too smooth, too perfectly balanced. An older part of my brain activates to tell me that this is wrong, uncanny. He's also taller, I think. He looks like how I remember him, but not.

He still has an infuriating smile plastered on his face, and I desperately want to claw it away. "You used to care what I liked."

"I hated pretending to be someone else to make you happy."

"Did you? I remember how happy you were when I was showering you with gifts, taking you to exclusive parties, pampering you at every opportunity. We were a golden couple, Ramona."

I sneer, but I can't think of anything witty to say.

I remember how the press adored us, the handsome heir to the largest corporation in North City, and his beautiful, smart girlfriend who was always wearing the latest fashions. Courtesy of him, of course. My family aren't gold-bloods, I couldn't have afforded any of it. Derek and I might as well have been old world royalty.

I'd been a bartender to pay my way through school when he met me and swept me off my feet with lavish gifts of fresh flowers and dinners out. He'd listened to all of my frustrations with my university classes, my professors, my projects —

charming me with his attentiveness. I've never been able to pinpoint exactly when it was that he revealed his true self, when he started asking me to change myself, no matter how many times I go over all my memories.

He takes my silence as an invitation and takes a half-step closer. His voice, after so long apart, is intoxicating. Part of me wonders if this is a new augment he has. "Do you remember the vacations we took, to the ocean? When we made love on the sand under the setting sun?"

I swallow hard. I'd shoved those memories away, along with everything else to do with him. His voice is unlocking them — the dreamy days of bliss where he whisked me off to any place I could think of, the parties spent in a happy sparkling haze of drink, his attentiveness to my pleasure when we were in bed.

He's smiling more broadly. "I know you remember. I knew you wouldn't be able to stay away forever. The second the sensors at the dark level went off that someone with augments had stepped into the building, I knew it was you. I flew here *tout de suite*."

Faintly, I hear Enix say, "What's happening? There's something weird going on with your biosigns Ro, what's happening?"

"If you hadn't come up to find my office, you might have gotten away with your little adventure, Ramona. This floor is a trap, specially made for you. What did you come to Scitek to find, hmm?"

He's so close I can feel the heat radiating off of him, and his face is tilted so that his warm breath is hitting my neck. I squeeze my eyes shut, hating that my body is betraying me, wanting him. My knees tremble, but I keep my mouth shut.

His hand reaches out and brushes my neck gently, sending shivers of pleasure down my spine. Damn him. Damn him to the deepest hells imaginable.

His thumb presses against my artery, finding the small bump of a microchip there and he pulls back, his face returning to a cold mask. "Good girl. You kept my special implant for you."

"No," I cry out and stumble back, released from the spell he's woven over me. It's too late, as he's tapping on the biocontroller on his wrist.

My scalp starts itching, and I know exactly what's about to happen. I scream, clutching at my head as the itching turns to blinding pain.

Embarrassment also floods me that this isn't the first time he's used the chip to change my appearance, or even the second. I had let him hurt me. I had let him rewrite my DNA to be something more of what he wanted.

In the far distance of my mind, I hear Enix exclaim, "This isn't possible! Ro's system is being flooded with targeted growth hormones, and I'm pretty sure genetic code modifications. There's no fucking way…"

"Hold on Ro," Tor is saying, "hold on."

"Stop it!" Ruby is saying. "Enix, do something!"

I can feel hair growing at an unnatural speed, sprouting out from my scalp in cascading waves. Instead of my natural dark hair, however, this new hair is pale blonde. I collapse onto my knees with my hands pressed against my scalp, sobbing in pain, unable to stop this from happening.

How had I been reduced to this again? How had I allowed myself to come back here? Did I really not know better than this?

Old shame roils in my stomach, and I retch between sobs.

Finally, the pain fades into a dull throbbing ache once the newly grown hair has reached my hips. I brace my hands on the ground, breathing heavily, trying to find some sort of centre. I feel Derek's hands in my hair, stroking it, and then there's the sound of scissors being pulled and he's gathering up my newly-grown hair and cutting it.

Scissors. He had planned for this. He came prepared.

Neon blue clumps of hair fall around me. I try to stop crying. I liked my blue hair.

When Derek lets go of my hair, I stay kneeling for a few seconds, reaching for the rekindled kernel of anger that burns brightly in my chest. When the urge to weep is safely tucked away, I shakily get to my feet, swiping my arm across my face to wipe away the tears.

Derek looks pleased with himself. "Much better. There's my model fiancée."

"I'm not your fiancée," I say raggedly, shoving the new hair out of my face. I want to tear it all out and set it on fire. I hate being blonde.

"You could come back," he says. "I invested a lot of money into you."

"No," I spit at him. "You invested money into making a doll you could use. You drugged me and had surgeons cut me up and remake me to your exact specifications."

This seems to bore him. "So? Humans age and their skin sags and they gain weight. I didn't want to see you lose your youth."

"You violated my body," I snap at him. "I didn't get a choice."

"Would you prefer that I had just dumped you for someone younger?"

"I wanted you to not be an asshole! You said you loved me, I thought that meant you loved me no matter what. Even if I started wrinkling and getting grey hairs."

Derek laughed. "How ridiculous. I'm wealthy enough to be a god. Why shouldn't I remake the world to my standards? I have no use for an ugly old crone as my companion."

I stare at him, blinding fury mingling with an old grief. I

stalk towards him. "You replaced my skin with synth-skin so it'll never show age marks. You made my breasts bigger, my waist smaller, my legs longer. You made me hairless except for my head, and you dictated the colour and length of my hair. God knows what else you had your scientists do to me on the operating table. There's barely anything left of me that is truly me!"

"I created perfection," he says, his eyes grazing over me. It feels like a desecration. "Why cry over what's lost when you can embrace the present? I gave you a gift."

"I'm so sorry, Ro," I hear Ruby whisper.

"If you don't kill him I will," Tor says.

"This explains so much," Enix mutters.

I punch at Derek, but he steps aside as easily as if he'd been expecting it. "You've gotten more enhancements since my scientists worked on you," he says casually, "but I've been working on myself, too."

With a guttural scream of rage, I launch myself at him, a flurry of kicks and punches that he blocks. It's with smug satisfaction that I see surprise flicker across his face as he is forced to move to avoid my strikes.

He stops talking, finally, as we begin a fast and furious exchange of blows, but he's on the defensive, stepping backwards towards the edge of the building. I grit my teeth, feeling the rush of endorphins that Enix floods my system with, mingling with my already spiked adrenaline. I could do this for hours. Derek thought he could take me on alone. He was wrong.

I drive him back until he hits the metal railing on the edge of the terrace, nowhere left to retreat to.

"Is this really what you want?" Derek says, no longer smiling, holding up his hands in surrender. "Are you going to kill your soulmate?"

"You're a sick bastard," I pant. "You didn't deserve my love."

"That's unfortunate," he says, but takes advantage of my pause to tap the biocontroller on his wrist. I can't move quick enough to stop him. Red hot needles shoot through my entire system, and I drop to the ground immediately, my muscles seizing.

Unable to speak, unable to move, I stare at him, mouth open like a god damn fish out of water. Set on fire and left to burn.

Derek grimaces, then kneels down next to me. "Ramona. What a waste. I had a failsafe installed when they were perfecting you, you know. So that if you turned out to be an ungrateful bitch, I'd be able to correct your behaviour. When you left the first time, it was so quick I didn't think to use it. But, you came back, just like I knew you would."

I can only gape at him, my eyes bulging out of my head. Enix is reciting my dropping oxygen readings like that will fix anything.

"You know, I asked to make the first cut. It was glorious to be the one to liberate you from your old shell, to start you on the path to perfection." He leans in closer. "I still think about it, the ease at which your skin parted under the scalpel, the trickle of blood, the thrill of it."

Revulsion crawls through me. I hate him with every fiber of my being.

My lungs have been frozen for too long; I'm losing my grip on reality. I can hear Ruby, Enix, and Tor screaming in my head, but I can't focus on their words.

My vision starts to go dark.

Derek taps his wrist and my body is released. I cough, gasping for air, as he gently touches my cheek with his hand. It's tempting to give into feral instincts and bite him like a rabid dog. "You know, you accused me of making you a doll. Perhaps that is your rightful role — to serve me. I spoiled you too much, I see that now. You need to be trained before you can be brought out in public."

He pulls his hand away before I can decide to use my teeth, but doesn't change his posture. I lie flat on my back, staring at him, trying to get my breath back. I will never let him take me again.

He shouldn't have let me live. He should have created more space between us. I shouldn't have come here.

With one quick swipe, the bodkin hidden in my forearm pops out and I slice it across his throat.

There's a moment of stillness where his face is frozen in a mask of surprise.

When time resumes its normal course, his hands move to clutch his neck as blood sprays out, covering me in a fine mist. I don't let him do anything else. I lash out with the bodkin, stabbing into the hateful controller on his wrist, a tingle of electricity jolting through my arm as it short-circuits.

His scream is more of a gurgle, and he tips over onto his side. I scramble up to my feet, still riding the high of my unbridled fury. Without thinking, I stomp into his face with my boot, over and over until his head is nothing more than a bloody pulp.

My throat feels raw, and I realize I've been screaming. I don't know who I am. My pants and boots are covered in grey matter and bone chips and blood. My stomach churns at what I've done.

That is when the shooting starts.

I whirl around. A squad of a dozen guards is fanned out, their assault rifles spraying me and my surroundings with bullets.

The bullets that hit my torso bounce off the skin-lattice, leaving only small holes in my synth skin, but some of the bullets catch me in the legs and the arms like sharp bites.

I don't want to die here with him. I would rather die in a literal gutter.

I throw myself off the side of the building.

For the briefest of moments, I feel weightless.

Then gravity catches me and yanks me down, and I'm

f
a
l
l
i
n
g
.

I roll over in the air so that I'm looking up at the stars.

My body feels heavy, and every part of me aches.

"How long until I hit terminal velocity?" I ask idly.

"What?" Ruby asks.

"I jumped off the side. How long until terminal velocity?"

"Jesus Christ the readings of your biosigns are insane," Enix breaks in. "I'm trying to compensate."

"I was shot," I say dreamily. Enix must be flooding me with dopamine or something, making me feel good. Some memory reminds me that most people who fall from a height actually die of terror long before they hit the ground. I guess with Enix at the controls I'll feel the splat. Oh well. "You know, the upside of falling is that the stars are really pretty from this angle."

"Ro, you have to get a grip on yourself. You won't survive the fall if you don't," Tor says.

I laugh. I sound hysterical. I don't care. "You all know what I am now. I've been modded past being human. I'm not even me, anymore. I'm some rich asshole's wet dream. I died a long time ago."

There's silence. Then I feel the synth skin on my arms peel back as Enix's latest mod invention kicks into life. Delicate, lightweight wings unfurl themselves, catching at the air. They're made of the same synthetic polymer of my skin-lattice — strong without being brittle, durable without being heavy.

It's only because of my bionetic skeleton that Enix even dared install them.

On instinct, I roll so that I'm facing down and spread my arms wide.

As the wings expand, the force against my shoulders is brutal and I grit my teeth against the pain. I can feel my fall slowing, though, and I fight to keep my arms out and flat, letting the wings catch against the air. I'm no longer plunging straight down but gliding through the night air.

It's strange to see North City from this angle. All the digital advertisements moving on the sides of buildings aren't meant to be seen from up here so they're more like hazy dreams. I can see the trams and pedestrians moving along the hive network of passageways between the buildings, but in miniature as if they're toys. It's pretty, in its own way.

Not the worst view to have as a last one.

Finally, the silence breaks.

"Is that how you think of me?" Enix's voice is gentle, patient.

"What?" The calmness of his voice startles me.

Enix, still steady, says, "I was experimented on until the authorities no longer considered me human enough. Am I not me?"

"Of course you are. That's not what I meant — you're still your own skin. I might as well be a doll. I'm not human. He didn't even leave me my own face."

"Ro, you're more than your body," Ruby says.

"That's easy enough for you to say," I say as the pressure of tears builds up behind my eyes. "You're human too. You aren't separate from your physical shell."

Some part of me knows that I'm howling at the injustice of everything that Derek did to me and lashing out because of it. That I'm angry at myself for having let him manipulate me into doing things for him of my own free will. I can't stop myself though. There are no masks, no filters left for me as I'm hanging in the sky.

Tor's voice is rock steady. "Fuck that. What is cybertermination, Ro?"

"The death of consciousness," I answer after a long pause. "The lingering of the body."

"If there's no consciousness, does the body matter?" Tor insists.

"No," I say, and the tears well up in my eyes, blurring everything. "No, it doesn't."

"Then you're still you and you're still alive. Are you really going to let him win?" Tor demands.

I hate Tor so much. The tears fully form and I'm crying once again. "No."

"Then snap out of it."

I scream wordlessly at the night air, every ounce of rage and grief I possess leaving my body, trailing behind me like a comet tail as I glide.

When a hollow sort of emptiness has settled into my chest, I take a deep breath, let it out, and refocus. "Enix, the wings work great."

"Hell yeah!" he exclaims, and I know he fist pumps the air even though I can't see it. I love him for it. "Told you my calculations were correct."

"I'm never doubting you again," I say, feeling fatigue scratching at the edges of my awareness. I know I'm still bleeding heavily, and its going to catch up to me eventually.

"I've sending the transport to rendezvous with your location," Ruby says, her voice bright. "Getting in will be a bit tricky, but we'll figure it out."

"Okay," I say.

We lapse into silence once more.

The haze of blood loss grows stronger, and my limbs feel leaden. It takes a lot of effort to keep my core engaged to keep my legs from dragging, and it's starting to get difficult. I want to close my eyes, more than anything in the world. It would be easy to simply pull my arms in and nose dive.

I focus on the riotous mix of glowing colours from all the digital displays that paint the night with light, the way it feels to soar like a bird above it all. It's a beautiful distraction.

Less than a minute later, the unmarked autopiloted transport is below me. Awkwardly, I try shifting my arms to learn how to change course, and after a few moments of trial and error, I've shifted my path to intercept the transport.

"Open the door," I say.

The door slides up and open, and I grab onto it with my hands, wincing at the feeling of the air pulling at my wings which are awkwardly caught in the wind stream of the transport. Gritting my teeth, I shift my grip so that I can press my cybernetics panel, and it is immediate relief as the wings quickly fold back into my arms and my synth skin slides back into place. I'm left clinging to the side of a transport, my stupid long hair buffeting me in the eyes and getting in my mouth.

I swing my legs into the transport, trusting in physics, and let go with my arms. Awkwardly, I land in a heap inside the transport and croak, "Close the door."

I lie sprawled across the seats of the transport for a long moment, laughing hysterically. I shouldn't be alive. Derek is dead. I *flew*.

"Ro, I'm still getting erratic biosignals," Enix says.

I lift my head and look at myself. "I'm bleeding. Three bullet wounds to the right thigh, two to the left, one to the upper left arm."

There's swearing, but I stop paying attention. None of the injuries hurt anymore. I feel warm, and the edges of my vision are soft and blurry. Now that I'm safe, my body relaxes, and I let my head loll back. "I'm so tired."

"Don't close your eyes, Ro," Tor says. "You have to stay with us."

"Mmkay," I say, closing my eyes. "Just for a second."

"No! Keep talking Ro," Tor insists.

"You're really annoying, do you know that?" I tell him.

"Good, be annoyed with me. I want you to tell me every day for the rest of my life how annoying I am."

"See, that's what I mean," I reply. "Only an annoying person would say that."

"Ro, tells us about the painting," Ruby breaks in.

"The painting?" I ask, puzzled. I'm only vaguely conscious of the feeling of the tube tucked against my lower back. "What about it?"

"What do you like about it?"

I sigh. Did I say I liked it? Maybe. I don't remember now. "We don't know if the subject was a real person, or a composite of multiple sitters. There's no record. The painter wasn't that well-known during his time. Isn't that funny? There are so many painters who only became famous after they died."

"What else?" Enix asks.

"The colours," I say drowsily. Is this actually important right now? "The painter used a very rare, expensive pigment for the blue of her head covering, the red of her lips. Did you know they used to crush bugs to make some colours? No one does that anymore."

"What was it like to hold the painting?" Tor asks.

I lie with my eyes shut for a long moment, resenting all of their questions. "It didn't feel real, even though it's the realest thing I've ever touched. You can see the individual brushstrokes. There are details that aren't visible in the digital recreations. It has a faint smell. I didn't expect that."

Vaguely, I'm aware that the transport has slowed, and when it finally stops completely the door slides open. I can't be bothered to move. "I'm stopped."

I don't have to try to get out because as soon as the door is open, Enix and Tor pull me out of the transport and lever me up on a gurney. Where they got one from, I have no idea.

"Hey," I say, blinking up at both of them.

Tor's eyes are red and puffy, and there's crusts of blood on his face and down his neck, but Enix's expression is grim as he starts attaching an IV line to my arm. Somehow, he has a blood transfusion pack, which is strange. When did he start storing blood?

Tor is holding bandages to my legs, trying to staunch the bleeding. Pain still only lives at the very edge of my awareness.

"I'm going to knock you out now," Enix says gently. "We're going to stich you up. With your increased healing factor, synth skin, and the blood transfusion, you'll be fine."

I limply wave my hand where the new microchip had been inserted at Scitek. "Can you get rid of this too?"

"Of course," Enix says. "I promise we'll take out the chip. I'm also going to take out the one in your neck, so no one will ever be able to use it again."

"Am I going to be stuck as a blonde?" I ask with a grimace.

"Probably," Enix says.

"Ugh. That's the worst part of all of this."

Tor makes a strangled sound.

"Shut up you." I glare at him. "I hate being blonde."

Ruby approaches, her hands clasped together tightly at her chest. She's also got dried blood on her face and in dark red tracks from her ears. "It'll be easier to dye. You won't have to bleach it."

I sigh heavily. "I guess you're right."

"Counting down. Okay Ro, five, four, three —"

My eyelids flutter, and I don't hear the rest of the count.

PART FOUR

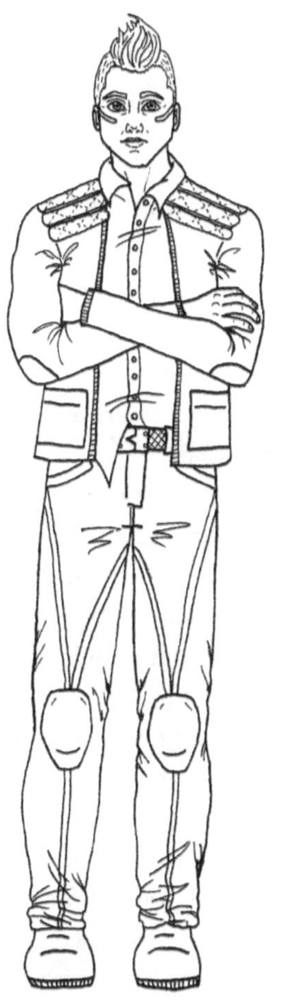

Consciousness returns slowly. I feel like I'm being dragged out of the deepest depths of the ocean when my eyelids peel open. As best as I can tell I'm still on the gurney, but back in our headquarters, Enix's lab.

My movement must have set off an alert as Enix wheels over to my side in his chair. "Hey! You're awake."

I grimace. "Do I have to be?"

Enix grins. "It's nice to hear your voice again."

The conversation snippets attract the attention of both Ruby and Tor, who appear to hover at my side.

"It's good to have you back," Ruby says, hands hidden in the sleeves of an oversized sweater. "I was worried about you."

"Yeah," Tor says, poetically.

"So what did I miss during my beauty sleep?"

"You've got missed messages from Rabbit," Ruby says.

"The city's in lockdown," Enix adds.

"Your face is all over the news," Tor says. "Your blood was all over the scene and you're wanted for murder."

I sigh heavily. "Well, I guess my cover as AgentLOL is blown. There's no way that Rabbit won't sell me out."

The others exchange glances.

"Yeah, that already happened," Ruby says.

"Cool. Okay. Any other bad news we want to get out of the way?" I ask. "Are we about to be arrested or beaten to death in five minutes?"

Enix shakes his head. "That's about the worst of it. I don't recommend reading the news articles about you though. They're not… flattering."

"They say you're experiencing cybersaturation-induced psychosis from having too many mods," Ruby says.

I roll my eyes. "Everyone who knows anything knows that that's not actually a real thing."

"You wanted to die for a minute there because you were convinced you weren't human enough," Tor reminds me.

I groan. "Aw come on, I just killed the world's worst ex-boyfriend, got shot multiple times, and threw myself off a building. I was just feeling a bit sorry for myself."

Tor leans over the gurney and scowls at me. "You're not going to get out of talking about it by being funny."

"You think I'm funny? That's the nicest thing you've ever said to me," I say and smile sweetly at him, batting my eyelashes.

He grumbles and leans back, crossing his arms. There's a secret smile hiding in the corner of his mouth, though.

Enix rolls his eyes. "Okay, if you two are done flirting, we do need to have a serious conversation."

That wipes the smile from my face. "What's the situation?"

"The money came through from Rabbit for the upfront payment for the painting. We also still have the painting, and we could sell it if we need more credits. I ran the payment through my usual random selection of accounts to obfuscate it," Ruby says. "But, with enough time, an AI might be able to trace the money from Rabbit to us."

"Okay."

"Your old and new faces are also plastered everywhere, and you're the city's number one most wanted criminal. They even have your folks on the news pleading for you to turn yourself in," Tor adds. "Unless you want to get more facial reconstruction, you will never be able to go out into public again as yourself. Your identity is so thoroughly compromised it's unsalvageable."

"Charming."

"The underworld knows who AgentLOL is now, so you're not even safe there," Tor continues. "Anyone worth their salt is going to hand you in for a reward."

I sigh heavily and sink back down into the pillow. "Couldn't you all have just left me in a coma for a month or so, until this blows over?"

"No," Enix says gently.

"What are our options, Ruby?" I ask, looking to our nethacker.

She grimaces. "Run."

"That's it?"

She nods.

My heart plummets. Running means leaving North City and trying to fend for ourselves out in the edges of habitable lands. Surviving on scraps, fighting the other fugitives for food, water, shelter. If we could steal an aircraft, we could make it to another city, but I know that that's not realistic — my name and face would have been sent to every other city on the god damn planet so that I can't find shelter anywhere.

I look at Enix, Ruby, and Tor in turn. "You three don't have to come. I'm the only one who's wanted, no one knows we're connected. You're all safe. I just ask that you help get me out of the city, and then you can live your lives with all the credits we've made."

They all exchange glances. This is clearly a topic they've discussed. Tor is the one who speaks. "As much as we appreciate your self-sacrificial streak, we agreed that we're in this together."

He hesitates, suddenly nervous, and says, "There's one other option."

I raise an eyebrow. "Oh?"

"The Union."

I glare at Ruby. "What criteria did I give you when I asked if you knew a good counter-AI hacker? No bleeding-heart do-gooders."

"Sorry, Ro. You asked for the best," she says with a sheepish shrug. "He's the best."

"Did you know about this too?" I ask Enix.

He smiles shyly. "Yeah."

"Now I know why you're always so smugly self-satisfied," I inform Tor.

He rubs his forehead with his hand, his expression one of frustration. "Can you take me seriously for just one minute, please."

I hold up my hands in surrender. "Okay, sorry. You asked nicely, so tell me about how the Union is better than scavenging for scraps in the wastelands."

Enix snorts, but stays silent.

Tor says, "For one, we'd still be in North City. I help them out sometimes, and they've got a network all through the city. They're gaining high-level support to push out the corporate governance bodies that dictate our lives, and have a government by the people, for the people."

I try not to roll my eyes.

"They'd be able to use all of us. Instead of stealing from the rich to line our pockets, we could make a real difference."

I raise an eyebrow. "I can see how you three can help

them, but what the hell am I supposed to do? I'm a wanted murderer with an art history degree. Also, they're never going to make a difference. Even if they do get a different form of government, what does that change? We're all still trapped in the oasis cities on a wasteland of a planet with nowhere to go."

"You're an experienced physical operative," Tor points out. "With a shitload of cybernetic enhancements. The Union isn't just talk. They take action too."

"I'm not going to become a professional killer," I say, crossing my arms.

"It's a shadow war, Ro. No one's asking you to become an assassin. Yeah, the planet's gone to hell, and that's shitty, but there's advancements being made in science and technology to reverse the climactic failures. The Union is actively testing some new inventions, and they look promising. But we can't go out of these cities under the yoke of corporate overlords. They're just going to install their old order that let the world burn to begin with. We need to make changes *now*, so that when it's time to leave North City, we do it in a way that benefits everyone. The Union doesn't pretend that their solution is perfect, but you can't let that be the enemy of progress."

"That's a hell of a speech," I say, studying Tor. I can tell he truly believes everything he said, down to his very core. His eyes are lit up, his expression open. It's the sincerest he's ever been, and I resent that he's hidden this side of himself until now. At least from me.

I rub an invisible stain on the white sheet covering me, buying time. I really don't want to try my odds out in the wide world. And I don't want to hide in the dark level waiting to die. I'm certainly not handing myself over to the police to experience a comedy of justice.

"Fuck it," I finally say. "Let's join the Union."

Tor smiles, and I swear it's the first time I've ever seen him truly happy.

"Fuck yeah," Enix says with a grin. "Welcome."

I stare at Enix, mouth gaping. "Seriously?"

He shrugs, but he doesn't look at all apologetic. "For years."

I whip my head around to stare accusingly at Ruby. "Don't tell me you're in on this too."

She smiles and shrugs. "Yeah. That's how Enix recruited me to the team."

I groan. "This explains why you all still live in such shitty apartments and are cryptic about your hobbies. Where do you even get the time?"

"You're not exactly a demanding boss," Enix says, leaning back in his chair, making it creak loudly. "We do a job together once a month or so?"

I feel like laughing. And crying too. "Why didn't any of you tell me?"

Tor seems to have gotten nominated as the one who tells me difficult things, as he says, "You weren't ready before."

"What do you mean?" I demand hotly.

"Ro, all you've been doing since you ran from Derek is hiding and living in the margins. I always wondered what you were hiding from." Tor's voice is gentle. "You don't go out except for jobs, you barely sleep, you barely eat. You jump at the slightest noise. You've been in a state of terror the whole time I've known you."

"Have not," I say, a lump in my throat. "No one who's scared starts working for the underworld."

"They do if they want to have a dry place to sleep and something to eat and not end up just another dead body tucked into a lost crevice of the dark level," Tor points out.

My body alternates between too hot and too cold. I look at Enix. The one I trust the most. "You could have told me."

Enix reaches out and grasps one of my hands in his two oversized palms. "Ro, you don't believe that it's possible to change who's in power. You never have. You accepted that the world is the way it is, and that we all need to deal with it. You never fought back. Until the rooftop."

Tears start sliding down my cheeks, and I hate it. I hate that I'm crying with an audience. Ruby grasps my other hand silently and gives it a sympathetic squeeze. I mumble, "I saw the full extent of power. I slept next to it. It's crushing."

Tor's expression is grim. "It is. But you're not alone. The whole purpose of the Union is that we're stronger together. One person alone can make themselves a martyr, but a thousand people together? That is also power."

I take my hands back and wipe my face, then look between all three of them. "I'm still mad at all of you for not telling me sooner. I'm also not convinced that this is going to amount to anything, but I'm willing to try."

"That's all we ask," Enix says gently.

I guess I can add another title to my collection — art historian, underworld thief, murderer, and resistance operative.

ACKNOWLEDGEMENTS

A lot of truly excellent people provided feedback to the making of this novella. Thank you to my alpha readers: Pat, Justine, and Nathaniel. Your initial feedback helped me structure this story into something I could see the promise in. Justine and Pat, thank you both for helping me brainstorm titles. I also owe a debt of gratitude to Rebecca, Christina, Kim, and Greg for being beta readers and pointing out places that I could strengthen the story. To my extended writing community — thank you for loving the first part of this story, and this little gang of characters.

ABOUT THE AUTHOR

Myka Silber grew up surrounded by the forests, mountains, and ocean of the Pacific Northwest. They now live in Ontario, Canada, with a mercurial cat and a bean of a dog. Myka holds both a BA and an MA in International Relations. They have previously published a short story collection and a novel, and you can follow them on Instagram @myka.silber.